Where the Sun
Never Sets

By

EMMA HAEL KIM

Gold Moose Publishing books may be purchased for educational, business, or sales promotional uses. For information, please email us at hyeay@hyeay.com.

ISBN: 978-1-969181-10-8

* The cover image for this book was created using an AI-based generative tool, Chat GPT. After being generated, the image was slightly edited and enhanced by a human.

Table of Contents

Where the Sun Never Sets

I should have seen this coming. I knew she wouldn't have kept her promise. I knew she couldn't be trusted, but I put my entire family's fate in her hands anyway.

Months before, I had been walking through the bustling marketplace by the coast, inhaling the pungent smell of dried seaweed and sweet melons that the hunchbacked grandmothers were selling. I had practically grown up at that market, spending more time here, peering at the fresh caught translucent squids that the toothless man sold, than at home, where I was supposed to be washing the blankets.

At home, I was expected to do all the chores as the daughter of the house would. Cooking, cleaning, tending to my father and brother. My mother had done these jobs before. When I was a little girl I would twirl around her, splashing the soapy water into the air, mesmerized by the droplets of water in the sun turning into jewels.

The crunching gray and white pebbles slowly gave way to tan sand, slightly darkened by the morning mist. I reached the end of the market, where there were a series of rock ledges jutting down to the beach below. With practiced precision, I jumped to each one, carefully avoiding the oval shaped boulder that would tip with the slightest bit of weight.

That time of the year, purple hibiscus flowers bloomed on the vines that clung to the high seaside cliffs, filling the air with floral scents every time a breeze passed. As I picked my way down the ledges, I plucked a flower.

Finally reaching the sandy shores, I took out a thinned muslin blanket and laid it out on the damp sand, careful to not get my skirt dirty. I sighed as I looked at the ocean, the waves pounding against the worn black rocks. Seagulls called to one another, flapping their onyx black tipped wings.

I sighed, plucking the light plum-colored petals of the hibiscus flower. The petals twisted and danced in the breeze, all eventually landing in the water, creating small blots of color on the blue expanse. The once-clear waters were now a murky slate gray. The big and loud Japanese boats had polluted the bay from frequent oil leaks.

My home, the coastal city of Busan, boasted the highest quality seafood in mainland Korea. All of this came to an end when the Japanese had occupied Korea. Their boats and commercial fishing scared away the fish, leaving the majority of the city jobless. Of course, the Japanese didn't care about that. The only thing they cared about was the land. The beautiful Korean peninsula, with fertile soil and clear skies. I drifted into a daydream, watching the waves break on the shore.

Suddenly, a young child came sprinting down the stretch of sand towards me. I stood up quickly when I realized it was Hyeon, the little boy who lived in the next cottage over.

"Hyeon! I've never seen you here before," I exclaimed. I frowned when I saw him panting. "Why did you run all this way?" I gave him a moment to catch his breath.

"Your dad... the soldiers...jail," Hyeon gasped, making wild gestures. Those words put together made the color from my face drain. I jumped up and began to run towards the other end of the beach.

Hyeon raced ahead of me, his little feet pattering on the gristly grains of wet sand. My heart thumped in my chest, drowning out every other sound. I barely took notice of the raindrops that had started to fall.

By the time I reached my house, my skirt and jacket were soaked through, reflecting the heaviness on my heart. I saw stone-faced soldiers cracking open the front door with their rifles.

"STOP!" I screamed. I had no idea why the Japanese were here. The soldiers glanced at me and smirked.

When the front door was finally splintered open, I ran inside.

"Father!" I sobbed, desperately running through the house. There was utter silence. My older brother, Jun, had gone out to work. He was a fisherman who worked on one of the few remaining Korean boats. Jun worked until night, so I knew he wouldn't be home.

The house was eerily silent, the air seeming to hang still. The sunset-tinged sunlight filtered through the blotchy decade-old rice paper screens, letting the floating dust catch light.

Suddenly, the door to the back broom closet creaked. While the soldiers ransacked the rest of the house, I shakily swung open the door.

The moment it opened, my father leaped out, screaming. He pointed a gun and fired, leaving a hole in the wall next to my head. All of the soldiers looked up as I screamed.

All of a sudden, soldiers swarmed around me, grabbing my father and dragging him outside. My hands shook as I brushed my hair out of my face. My tight braid had come loose, my baby hairs floating around my temples like a halo. I was so confused. Why were there soldiers storming into my house, taking my father?

My father! I couldn't lose him, too! I had to protect him. I ran outside, nearly tripping on an overturned vase. If I lost my father as well, Jun would never forgive me. I could never forgive myself.

When I was a few years younger, I had been home with my mother. Jun and my father were out on my uncle's fishing boat, because Jun had wanted to bring home a fish for Mom. Mom had been feeling sick lately, so that night she had been brewing gukhwa-cha. The fragrant chrysanthemum tea filled the house with a honey scent.

"Soojin-a, do you think Jun will catch a fish?" My mother asked, giddy at the prospect of having a whole fish for dinner. Because my father had become crippled a few years earlier, he could not work. Soon, our family's money and prospects dwindled, and we eventually had to take scrap donations from our neighbors, or the leftovers from the market for food. My younger self had glared at the pouring rain.

"No." I said, jealous that my older brother had done something to make my ailing mother smile. In those days, my mother's eyesight had started failing, and she started dropping and tripping on things. To cheer her up, my father and older brother went out to try and catch a cod for Maeun-tang, her favorite soup. I left the lantern burning low on the kitchen counter, its dim golden light casting sleepy shadows across the walls. The rain had started up again—not a downpour, but the kind that drapes itself over the world like a veil, soft and persistent, whispering in the dark. I slipped on my sandals and pulled the hem of my nightdress into my coat. The cold had teeth tonight, and it bit at my ankles as I stepped out of the house.

The cliffs weren't far—just past the stone garden, beyond the row of wind-warped cypresses. I walked slowly, the wet leaves sticking to the soles of my feet, the air heavy with petrichor and memory. The purple hibiscus always grew wild there, clinging to the edge like they knew the danger and bloomed defiantly anyway. My mother loved them.

Earlier that evening, I had watched Jun tie a piece of ribbon that he had found around a beach rose. She kissed his forehead and smiled in that quiet, full way she does when she's trying not to cry. I had stood at the kitchen door with my hands behind my back, pretending not to notice. But I did. I noticed how her eyes softened. I noticed how she kept touching the ribbon even after he'd run off. I wanted to give her something too—something she hadn't asked for but would hold onto. I told myself it was only fair.

The flowers were heavy with rain, their petals dark and trembling under each drop. I picked them carefully, the cliffside slick with mud.

Back home, I could still smell the chrysanthemum tea. It had been on the stove since before I left, forgotten now, its scent growing dark and bitter. I didn't move to take it off. I assumed my mother went to the market, not even thinking about what she could be doing. The flowers in my hands were trembling— I told myself it was the wind.

I sat on the floor, near the hearth, threading the stems into a crown the way my mother taught me. One loop, one twist, tuck the stem behind. Again. Again. My fingers were clumsy with cold.

I held the finished flower crown in my little 8-year-old hands, smiling smugly at the fact that Umma had something to smile about from me, too. I fell asleep waiting for my mother. She never came back.

Now, I couldn't breathe. I gripped my dress, the fabric bunching in my sweaty, trembling hands. I rolled the vase back up and ran outside. The soldiers had clustered around my father and were yelling and laughing in Japanese.

"Hey! Stay away from him! Please! He's just an old man!" I shrieked, my voice coming out distorted.

The soldiers momentarily looked up, confused. They burst out laughing.

"You little Joseon dog!" they laughed, turning back to my father. I clawed my way through them and saw my father laying in the dirt in a fetal position. His worn homespun tunic was filthy and torn, and blood flowed freely from his temple. My eyes burned, my last tears spent.

I lunged toward the nearest soldier, my hands clawing at his face. How dare they? They invade our peaceful country, put my brother out of business, then hurt my father. I wanted to kill them all.

The soldier punched me, and I fell. Others swarmed around, and I could feel their red-hot kicks and punches. Vision was going black at the edges. I reached out to my neighbors, seeing if anyone would help, but they had disappeared into their own houses. Just as I was about to faint, the beatings stopped.

I looked up. Silhouetted from the sun overhead, the soldier's face cast long shadows. His slitty eyes glared at me. I defiantly met his eyes, determined to not feel lesser than him.

"Well, well. It looks like the daughter of a criminal is no better than him!" the man scoffed, earning a round of laughter from the officers. I bit back more tears as I reached out to clench my unmoving father's hand. When the man turned to meet the eyes of his officers, all of the men stopped laughing and stood at attention.

"Why are you doing this?" I asked. I was truly curious. Why had they just barged in and started beating me and my father? If anyone was guilty, surely it was the Hwang family two doors down. Mr. Hwang had been teaching lessons of Korean literature and history to his children and friends. Just studying the Korean alphabet could earn someone fifty days in jail!

"Oh? This is a surprise. Now, Mr. Sun, one would think that you would at least tell your dear daughter about—" The captain was cut off as a high-pitched gasp filled the street. Standing a few feet away from my father was a young woman dressed in a flowing crimson kimono, followed by maids gently waving lotus fans. The woman bounded over to us, her fluffed chignon bouncing with every step she took.

"What is this? What? Captain Tanaka, explain!" When I looked closer, the young woman was really more a girl about my age. The girl had her arms crossed and looked furious.

"Well? Speak! Do you not see this poor man lying in the middle of the street?" the girl exclaimed, stomping her foot. My jaw dropped. How did she speak like that and not get reprimanded?

The Captain opened his mouth and closed it again. I almost laughed at him looking like a fish out of water. I stood up and brushed the dust off my skirt. Much to my surprise, the girl ran to my side and held my arm up.

"Oh gosh, I'm so sorry! Let me help you get cleaned up." The girl dragged me towards her procession of maids and handed me a ceramic chalice of scented water. I held the goblet with wonder, never having smelled such a wonderful fragrance in my life. The water smelled of summer, with a soft rose scent layered over a bright orange blossom. Afraid to tarnish the smooth porcelain with my dirty fingers, I quickly placed it on a silver tray that one of the maids was holding.

The girl fluttered over to a guard standing behind the maids and ordered him to help my father up. The guard obeyed and carried him, walking up the hill towards the recently built mansion meant for the new Japanese governor. I tried to follow them, but the girl stopped me.

"My name is Hanako." She said, extending her uncalloused white hand towards mine. I clenched my skirt, trying to avoid touching her. I was so sure that she had some sort of hidden motive.

The girl- Hanako- dropped her hand when she realized I wasn't going to shake it. She instead linked arms with me and dragged me up the hill, following her guard and my father.

"So," Hanako said, "How would you like me to punish the Captain?" I stopped in my tracks and gaped at her.

"Pardon?" I asked, unsure if I heard her correctly.

"Well, that Captain is known for his impulsive and abusive behavior, but beating an innocent old man is shallow, even for him."

"W-well, I don't think it's very appropriate for someone like me to punish him." At this comment, Hanako looked sternly into my eyes. Hers were an icy sort of onyx.

"What do you mean, someone like you?"

"Um. A Korean person?" I said meekly.

"Well, since we're friends now, you can do that kind of thing."

"Friends?" I stared at her smiling face. At this point, I was so sure that she had gone crazy. Hanako was seemingly defying all of the social rules and expectations without the bat of an eye.

I looked up and saw that I had been lagging behind. Hanako was at the top of the hill, waiting for me. Not wanting to rudely waste her time, I hiked my skirts up and raced after her.

At the top of the hill, the mansion looked even bigger. The sky seemed to be struggling to make room for the massive red doors that served as a gate to the outer courtyard. With a flick of her hand, two armed guards signaled for the gates to open.

When the doors finally heaved open, I was overwhelmed by the sight of the house. Rows and rows of blooming pink azaleas gave a burst of color and a subtle sweetness within the beautiful artwork of strategically placed red pine trees. A well-maintained white gravel path lined with sculptures of volcanic rock stretched to the gleaming marble staircase of the ladies inner quarters.

I hurried on after Hanako as she calmly ordered her procession of maids to open the light tan bamboo screens. When the screens slid open, I rushed to slip her lacquered sandals off her feet. As I reached down, Hanako yelped.

"Ah! What are you doing?" She said, staring inquisitively at my hands.

"Um, I'm taking off your sandals." I said, unsure why she was oblivious. Korean girls like me were supposed to serve the Japanese girls. It wasn't a law, but it was the expectation.

"I've told you before, you're my friend. You don't need to do anything," Hanako laughed.

"In fact, I wanted to do something fun with you!"

I stared at her, my thought process ending when she said, "you don't need to do anything." I decided to play it safe while I had the chance and followed her down the ornately decorated hallway with a smile plastered on my face.

I felt heat radiating to my feet, and with much shock realized that the inlaid wooden floors must be heated. When I looked down, I saw my filthy bare feet making faint dirt marks on the polished floors. I tugged my skirt down in red-faced embarrassment. I noticed that Hanako's foot maids were dressed better than me, with their pristine linen robes and whittled mahogany hair sticks. Suddenly, I felt self-conscious and ashamed of my ragged hemp skirt and jacket, the color faded to a dull brown instead of the white that it was meant to be.

"Here we are!" Hanako skipped back to me. I quickly stopped trying to make my skirt longer and looked up. Hanako had led me into a spacious balcony overlooking the ocean. It had a floor that was seemingly made of one piece of smooth rock, and the balcony railing was made with glass panels, precariously placed directly over a vast park with many flowers and sculptures.

"What is this place?" I said under my breath. Hanako looked like she even had a private beach for herself.

"Hm? What was that?" Hanako asked, while bringing over a set of snow-white robes. She tossed one to me, and I almost dropped it at the softness. I ran my hand over the material again and again, still not daring to guess what it was made of. After slipping it on, I still couldn't get over the texture.

"What am I supposed to do?" I finally asked after a long moment of awkward silence. I had been fidgeting in the corner, while Hanako sat on one of the benches with a nail file.

"I'm so glad you asked! I was starting to get worried that you maybe didn't want to do it."

"Do what?" I was asking lots of questions lately.

"A makeover of course! What did you think?" Hanako gestures to the crates neatly organized with hairbrushes, nail polish, and other makeup. She grabbed my wrist and pulled me over to the first crate which was filled with ceramic pots that were the size of my hand.

"First we're going to do a relaxing water pressure therapy, so grab the soap and let's go!" Hanako grabbed a blue pot with a lotus on it, so I quickly picked up the same one before Hanako could drag me away again.

"I'm so excited to see the results!" Hanako said as two maids sat us down on stone benches in a dimly lit stone room.

"What results?" I asked, still holding the rose scented soap to my face, inhaling its fragrance. The soft scent made my nose tingle.

"Oh, I just meant I can't wait to see what you'll look like under all of that dirt and grime," Hanako explained, dipping her fingers into the giant steaming tub of rice water. When I heard that, I stopped admiring the pale pink color of the soap bar and stared at her.

"What?" I blinked, stunned.

"I can see how you could look good, and I'm going to take up responsibility by fixing you!" She said happily, flicking the warm rice water towards me.

11

"*Fixing me?*" I almost laughed. Of course. She was just like any other Japanese person. She had probably used the "friend" act to get me to be her personal punching bag later. I placed the bar of soap back in the ceramic pot and stood up. I bowed and was about to walk out.

"Where are you going? Was the temperature not to your liking? I can have the maids change it." Hanako stood up as well and waved a maid over.

"No, I just didn't want to dirty your precious robes with my filthy face, my lady," I smiled then frowned. I heaved the door open and walked out. How could I have been so stupid? Of course she wasn't trying to be nice.

I spun on my heel, threw on my old and dirty hemp skirt and jacket when I realized that I was still wearing Hanako's robes, leaving them neatly folded on a side table near the door to the women's quarters. I marched around the trim gardens in search of my father. Spotting a small house-like structure near the side of the mansion, I ran toward the door.

I knocked and heard a shuffle and a crash. The door opened to an apologetic young man in sun-bleached gray pants and a white tunic clutching gardening tools.

"Hello," I said in Korean, assuming he was hired by the governor. It was unlikely that he was Japanese because he was wearing commoner's clothes.

"Hi, may I ask who you are and why you knocked?" He asked, replying in Korean, setting his tools down with a clatter on a sagging wooden table near the doorway.

"Oh, well my name is Sun Soojin, and I am looking for my father." I said, bowing slightly in greeting. The young man didn't seem much older than me, and his easy-going laid-back personality was disarmingly friendly.

"Oh! Is your father the person Tsuyoshi was carrying? The poor man! What happened?"

"Some soldiers decided to gang up on him for some reason and started beating him up!" I cried, letting my anger pour out. "I mean, he was innocent! Minding his own business and all that."

"Ugh, I can't believe they would do that to someone just because." We were talking in low voices, with our heads together in fear that someone would hear us. I sighed.

"Anyway, who are you?" I asked, realizing he had never introduced himself to me. Realizing this as well, the young man bowed his head.

"I'm Hanjun and I am the assistant gardener here at the respectable Sato household. Welcome to my humble abode." As he said the last sentence, a shovel fell over with a clang somewhere in the shed and Hanjun winced.

"Do you want me to help you find your father?" Hanjun asked.

"Please! This place is so huge that if I got lost, I probably wouldn't be found until a week later!" Hanjun laughed at this and motioned for me to follow him.

He led me around to the back lawn. Tall trees made a pathway to a glistening lake, complete with lotus flowers bursting everywhere along the edges, with cattails shooting up between the pink and white clusters.

"It's so beautiful here. I can't imagine having a lake to yourself," I said, marveling at the greenery's breathtaking beauty.

"Oh, haha. On the weekends, me and my small army of gardeners take three whole days just to fix up the edges of it." Hanjun shrugged as he helped me climb the stone steps of a chamber that faced the lake. He slid the light wooden frame open and motioned inside.

"Is this where my father is?" I questioned. I knew my father would much rather be lying in the street than be in the proximity of a Japanese person.

"Yes, I saw Tsuyoshi carrying him in here. He's the guard." Hanjun clarified as I walked through the dimly lit hallway. The corridor had a musky and spicy scent, like one of those expensive perfumes that merchants from the west were selling. I wondered how many bottles the governor had bought to make the entire place smell so strongly of the fragrance.

We arrived at a doorway with ornately carved lotus flowers and a guard standing by the door. I recognized him as the one who carried my father up the hill.

"Miss Sun, your father is resting in this room," he said gruffly in Japanese, sliding the door open for me and Hanjun.

"The master usually lets his formal guests use this space, but he is away today, and Miss Sato insisted." Hearing this, I instantly thought about how I had just left Hanako standing while I walked out on her. Pushing the uncomfortable thought aside, I quickly stepped through the frame. On an elevated pallet surrounded by flowering lilies was my father, his head resting on a soft-looking pillow. For a second, an icy feeling washed over me as I wondered if he was dead or alive.

"Father?" I whispered, gently shaking his shoulders. I was about to shake him a bit harder when his eyes snapped open. At first, his eyes were hazy and unfocused, but as soon as they landed on my worried face, he came back to consciousness.

"I'm not dead yet, dear daughter. Unfortunately, I still have 30 or so years left," My father chuckled and then became serious.

"What is this place? Where are my crutches?" He asked, hopping out onto the floor and looking around. His right leg was permanently crippled due to a full wagon running over it when he was a small child.

"This is the governor's house, father. A guard brought you here to heal after he saw what those people were doing to you." I left the part about Hanako out on purpose to save my father at least a shred of dignity.

"What?! Heal? I'm perfectly fine, thank you very much!" He shouted as he snatched his two walking sticks from a woven basket near the windows that overlooked the lake. He leaned heavily on them as he hobbled out as fast as he could. He needed help getting down the stairs, and I tried grabbing his left crutch to steady him.

"Get me out of here!" He snapped at Hanjun, who obviously knew the way better than me. I followed behind, desperate to explain. However, the more that I thought about it, I realized I truly had no good answer. The moment Hanako introduced herself, no, the moment I saw her ordering her guard to pick up my father I knew I should have objected. The second I accepted any help would mean our family would fall into some sort of debt. Not to mention, my father in particular hated the Japanese more than anything.

Guilt filled me as I thought back on how I almost let myself be befriended by the daughter of the Japanese governor while my poor beaten father was lying injured and alone somewhere.

Hanjun had a quick word with the guards at the outer gate while my father stood still, waiting for them to open.

"Hanjun, thank you so much for everything. I hope we can meet again!" I said to him apologetically as he waved to me.

"No worries! I'm glad you found your father!" Hanjun smiled worriedly and ushered us through the giant red gates.

My father's face was contorted into something filled with rage and embarrassment, the mix of those two being the most dangerous to be around. As soon as the gates heaved open, my father stormed through. He went down the hill at a dangerous speed, not stopping until he reached our house.

"Be careful, don't fall!" I called after him. My father just kept hobbling towards the house.

"Soojin!" A furious voice roared from inside. I gulped. If my brother was yelling, it was definitely not good. I reached for the handle, but the door pulled itself open. On the other side, my older brother looked like he was about to explode.

"What is this? Can you not see that the house has been ransacked? Do you know how worried I was when Father wasn't home? No! Of course you wouldn't! Not when the neighbors see you going into that bastard governor's mansion without a second thought!" Jun, my older brother, yelled until his face was redder than the fireball of the setting sun. After about 20 minutes of furious ranting, Jun finally quieted and took care of our exhausted and angry father.

I started to move the intact pieces of the few of our furniture that remained, desperate to be helpful. Jun was busy tending to our father's every need, constantly getting up to fix his blankets or get fresh rags for his injuries.

"I'm sorry," I finally muttered, sorting through a pile of broken chairs. Jun passed by, not even glancing at me. He slammed the sliding door, returning to his usual cold, unresponsive self.

"The governor's guards took good care of Father, you know," I said into the empty air, trying to further convince myself that leaving my unconscious father in our enemy's house wasn't totally bad. I was glad that I hadn't slipped and told Jun and my father about Hanako. The two would be even more furious and maybe never let me out of the house again. Worse, if the village found out, our family would be outcasts.

I curled up on the floor, replaying all the things that had happened. Who would have thought that I, a poor girl from a backwater village, would even set foot in a Japanese governor's mansion? Even more shockingly, receive an invitation for a friendship with a noble's daughter? I shivered on the cold floor, my sleeping pallet torn and abandoned from the ransacking earlier that day. The chilly autumn air seeped through the splintered screens and carried me back to the night my mother died.

On that night, when I had fallen asleep on the cold floor like this, my mother had gone out looking for me. I had taken a shortcut through the woods to the cliffside, while my mother went the long way. A few months prior, she had started constantly feeling weak and clumsy. She fell often and could not get up by herself. Furthermore, her vision had started to deteriorate, making it so that she couldn't make her way around the house in the evening. That night, it had been raining hard, making the soft earth near the cliff incredibly slippery. While my mother was calling my name into the downpour, she tripped on an overturned rock and slid off the cliff. Later that morning, marks at the edge of the cliff had indicated that she had struggled to stay hanging on. Eventually, she plummeted down onto the sharp rocks that rose out of the ocean. They found her lifeless body in the water near where the fishing boats were anchored.

My father had tried to forgive me, knowing that a small child couldn't have known. Still, he flinched whenever he looked at me, and I could see that it was hard for him to take care of me. Jun on the other hand, once a vibrant and talkative older brother, turned his back, not speaking to me for weeks. He stayed this way, and the three of us eventually drifted apart over the years.

I drifted off on the cold floor, still thinking about how different it could've been if I had just stayed home that night.

The next morning, I woke to the sound of tapping. The noise was quiet and soft, but also rapid. At first, I thought it was a woodpecker, but then the noise became louder. I opened my tired eyes and lifted myself up onto my elbows.

"Oww," I groaned. The cold floors had given me cramps up and down my joints. Still bleary and disoriented, I rubbed my face and blinked toward the door. The tapping came again— more deliberate this time. Someone was knocking. I staggered to my feet, wrapped the blanket around my shoulders like a shawl, and shuffled across the room. When I opened the door, a maid in a familiar uniform stood there, perfectly composed with Tsuyoshi the guard a few steps behind her. Her hands were folded neatly in front of her, holding a pale lavender envelope sealed with gold wax. Even through the haze of sleep, I could tell this wasn't an ordinary note.

"For you, Miss Sun," she said politely in accented Korean, bowing slightly as she extended the letter. I blinked at her, still half in a dream. My fingers closed around the envelope, but I couldn't bring myself to speak. Everything felt surreal—the cold, the letter, the maid's presence at my door. She waited a beat and then bowed slightly again.

"It's from Lady Hanako."

I blinked.

"Huh?" I sputtered, eyes widening. Why would Hanako send a letter? All of the color drained from my face as I thought of a possibility; what if she was mad that I walked out on her, and now she was letting me know that she would punish my family? With a shaking hand, I took the letter from the maid.

Carefully working my nails under the pressed wax, I opened the crisp letter. I expected threats and punishments, but to my surprise, it was quite the opposite. In refined Japanese, the note read,

Soojin,

I hope this note reaches you in good spirits. I wanted to write because I have been reflecting on our conversation, and I fear I may have spoken out of turn. If I said anything very improper to you, please accept my sincerest apologies. I only meant to be honest, but I may have said so harshly.

If you are willing, I thought maybe we could go for a walk together later this afternoon. Just to talk. No pressure, of course—I understand if you decline.

Warmly,

Sato Hanako

I reread the letter, slower this time. She was… apologizing? Or at least trying to. There was no sarcasm, no stiff formality. Just an awkward sort of honesty. I didn't know what to make of it. For a moment, I considered tossing it aside. I even held it loosely in my hand like I might let it slip into the waste bin. It wasn't like she'd begged me to stay before or seemed especially sorry. And yet… she had taken the time to write. I glanced down at the note again. It almost seemed nervous. It wasn't much, but at least she had tried something. And, if I was being honest, walking out probably hadn't been the most graceful move on my part either. With a quiet sigh, I folded the letter back up and tucked it away. Maybe I'd go. Just to hear her out.

Sighing, I knotted a clean skirt around my chest and pulled my cropped jacket over my shoulders. Gathering my mess of black hair into a braid, I sighed again.

"Why today of all days?" I groaned. My hair was tangled and my skin blotchy from pressing against the floor. I imagined that Hanako was all dressed up in another one of her silk kimonos, her hair piled into a chignon on her head and her face powdered. All served by people like me.

The walk to the park felt longer than usual, like the air itself was dragging at my ankles. I kept thinking about the letter, trying to pin down her tone. When I finally spotted her near the low stone fountain, my steps slowed. She wasn't dressed like she had been the day before. No flowy extra robes, her hair tied back in a simple bun. I blinked, unsure if I was more surprised or relieved. It made her look younger, like she'd stepped down from some pedestal I didn't even know I'd put her on.

She turned at the sound of my shoes on the gravel path and gave a hesitant smile.

"Oh hi!" she said, exclaiming, "You came!"

"Yes. I wasn't sure I would," I answered honestly. We sat on a bench under a creaky gingko tree, the early afternoon sun flickering through the branches. For a few seconds, neither of us said anything. Then she started talking—about the letter, about how she hadn't known how to reach me. I nodded along, my fingers pulling at a loose thread in my sleeve. The conversation moved, but awkwardly. Stilted pauses, small apologies, sentences that trailed off. It felt like we were both trying to translate something from two completely different languages—hers built on intentions, mine on experience.

Just as Hanako was about to say something else, I saw movement in the corner of my eye. I turned.

Nari and Hayun. They were across the path, half-hidden by a dogwood tree, frozen mid-step. Both were staring at us—no, at *me*. Their expressions twisted in a strange mix of shock and... concern? Nari looked like she wanted to say something, but Hayun touched her arm and shook her head. They just stood there. Wisps of hair escaped from Hayun's long brown braid and floated around her temples like a halo. Nari blew her short-cropped black bangs out of her eyes in disbelief. Ever since we were all ten years old, Hayun still refused to wear any other color skirt than pink, and Nari still hadn't grown out of her baby face.

My stomach dropped. They *saw* me. With Hanako. Nari squinted her eyes and leaned towards Hayun, whispering something in her ear. Hayun nodded, and both paled. I clenched my teeth and drew in a sharp breath. They didn't know Hanako personally, but the new governor and his daughter had been introduced to the whole city a few weeks prior.

I turned back to Hanako quickly, as if by ignoring them I could erase their presence entirely. But the weight of their gaze remained.

"Is... something wrong?" Hanako asked, noticing the shift in me.

"Um, no, it's fine," I laughed shakily. I turned my body away from the trees to block Hanako from spotting Nari and Hayun.

"I-I'm sorry for walking out on you that day," I said quickly.

"I just felt really shocked, and after all the things that happened earlier in the day I got in my head," I sighed. I hope she was planning on forgiving me.

"It's fine. I thought about it, and I realized that I could have really hurt you. I didn't mean it that way. I was just saying what was on my mind first. I never really think about what I say, and that's something I need to fix," Hanako said, fidgeting. I noticed that she was avoiding eye contact.

I breathed a sigh of relief, knowing that most of the confusion would be over. Just then, a young maid hurried over.

"Miss Sato, your father is summoning you back to the manor. It would be best to leave now," she said, bowing her head.

"Well, I guess I'll have to see you some other time, Soojin. Oh, and by the way, you can just call me Hanako. It would be way too uncomfortable for me to hear you say lady or miss."

Hanako stood up and brushed her skirt. I stood with her, stretching. We had been sitting on a bench for a long time, and my legs had gone stiff.

"I'm so glad we could clear this up, miss- I mean, Hanako," I said, her name sounding clunky in my mouth. At this, Hanako smiled.

"Me too," She squealed, back to her bubbly self.

"We have to see each other again soon! Bye!" She called, waving. I smiled and gave her a little wave back, and then quickly put my hand down. I still was being careful in public, still scared about what Jun had said the night before. Confirming that none had been watching, I shook my head. I shuddered as I imagined word getting to the old ladies who were famous for their

22

gossiping and bartering at the markets. If even one of them heard, the whole region would know by the end of the day.

I turned, only to find the glaring faces of Hayun and Nari inches from my own.

"Ah!" I cried, nearly tripping on the bench behind me. Had they been watching me the entire time?

"What were you doing? And don't say that it's nothing," Nari glared. She was the only daughter in a house with four older brothers and acted like them. No one in the village dared to say anything to her in fear of getting jumped by her brothers later.

"I recognize that girl. Who is she? Soojin, answer us!" Nari placed her hands on her hips and looked to Hayun for support. Hayun was playing with her hair, looking conflicted. She was the shyest out of the three of us. Her mother had practically raised Hayun by herself ever since her husband had left the two of them for a new life up north.

"What do you mean? I-I don't know what you're talking about," I feigned innocence. I knew I was horrible at lying, and I winced as even Hayun rolled her eyes.

"Soojin, I think you're better off just telling us straight out..." She said gently. Even Hayun, who was always soft spoken and kind, looked troubled.

I sighed.

"Fine, I'll tell you. She's Sato Hanako, the governor's daughter," I exhaled.

Nari exploded, "What?"

"Wait, isn't she the girl everyone was talking about?" Hayun questioned.

"Well, yes," I started. By 'everyone,' Hayun meant the group of girls who hung around the docks. A few days after the Governor had arrived, word got around about his daughter. The girl who wore dresses and kimonos made only of silk, and who had at least 5 maids to wait on her every single day.

"Why? Did she offer you money? Did you have to repay something?" Nari scoffed, clearly shocked.

"No... She just asked me if I wanted to hang out," I started, but Nari cut me off.

"Didn't you know that we have to pay an even higher tax because of them? The Governor's spoiled daughter is sooo high maintenance that we're struggling to feed ourselves while she's throwing away gold bars!" Nari yelled. She had been obviously listening to one of her older brother's rants.

Hayun grimaced but didn't say anything.

"How was I supposed to know about the taxes? You know Jun doesn't speak to me anymore!" I shouted back at Nari. I wondered how she could have been so inconsiderate.

"Well, you should at least know that speaking a word to that girl is considered a betrayal!"

"What? She asked, and I answered!"

"Ha! What are you, that girl's servant?"

"Stop calling her 'that girl!' Her name is Hanako!"

Hayun stepped between us, and shouted, "Stop! Both of you just stop it! Screaming your heads off isn't going to solve anything, and both of you should be ashamed of yourselves! We're supposed to be friends, and here we are, fighting over a random girl!"

I quieted, stunned. In all the years I had known Hayun, she had never been this up-front and loud.

"I-" Starting to speak, I stepped towards Hayun but she firmly held out her hand.

"No. I don't know what got into you but I'm going to keep my distance from now on. I don't need any unnecessary trouble coming to me and my mother. We can talk again after you've come to your senses." With that, Hayun walked away. Nari gave me one more glare before running to catch up with Hayun.

My mind finally grasped the situation as I watched the silhouette of my two best friends slowly becoming smaller in the distance.

I watched them leave until I couldn't see them anymore and then, turning back to the bench, exhaled the breath that I had subconsciously been holding. My best friends had left me, because of Hanako? I almost laughed out loud, then felt tears threatening to spill. It wasn't fair. I was allowed to have other friends besides them, too.

I thought about what Hanako would say to this. She would probably grow indignant and demand that Nari and Hayun reconsider.

I had way too much free time, now that my father and Jun were almost always out of the house, avoiding me. Even my family had distanced themselves from me. I collapsed back on the bench and replayed the scene over and over. Nari and I yelling, Hayun silencing us both, then me. Alone.

Again, my situation reminded me of when my mother had died. Much like the last few days, my father and brother had avoided me then as well. I was the main reason my mother was gone and that was when Jun had stopped speaking to me. Before, he had been my best friend. After that night, Jun almost seemed scared of me. As time went by, his fear turned into anger, then resentment.

My father on the other hand, had had his heart shattered. Father and mother had been childhood friends as well, so he had lost a lifelong partner. For a few months he would look at me with a melancholy gaze. However, as more time passed, he came around and went back to normal.

As the village was small, word got around faster than the scent of rice cooking in the winter. I had no one to play with, as the families in the village kept their children away from me. At the market, I was unspokenly labeled as 'the girl who killed her mother.' The only person who didn't judge me for that was the grandmother who sold crabs on the corner. The only reason she didn't know was because she was deaf. During this time, Hyun and Nari were the only girls who would play with me.

I stood up and started to head home. Only a single line of orange could be seen on the horizon, and the stars were starting to come out.

It had been a week since I last stepped out of the house. The timing was perfect, because Jun was gone on a fishing gig for a month, and my father had decided to disappear to one of his friend's houses. Eating nothing but dried squid all week, I had definitely lost weight, and now my skirt and jacket looked draped over my body.

"This isn't right," I muttered to myself as I yanked my fingers through clumps of hair. It wasn't fair that my friends and family would leave me over a new friend. Wrestling my hair into a braid, I trudged up the hill.

I exhaled in front of the big red gates. Surprisingly, the guards didn't stop me as I asked to see Hanako.

"Uh, I was wondering if I could see Ha- I mean, Lady Hanako today," I said quietly in Japanese, not being able to look the armored man in the eye. The guard looked at his partner and nodded.

"Lady Hanako will be out in a moment, miss," The guard said gruffly, stepping back into his place.

In a moment, Hanako's eager face popped out from behind the red gates.

"Hi!" She exclaimed, back to her usual self. I smiled weakly and gave a small wave.

"Are you ok?" Hanako asked, noticing something off.

"Um, yeah. Can we go somewhere?" I asked, eyeing the maids trailing behind Hanako.

"Yeah! Did you have anywhere in mind?" She asked, motioning for the procession of people to fall back.

"How would you like to visit the market?" I turned to face her defiantly. If I really was going to go through with this, I might as well have confidence. In the back, one of the maids looked up, concerned.

"There's a market?" Hanako asked, brightening. I was only shocked for a second, as the market was the center of the town and social life for the villagers. Then I realized that Hanako had no reason to go herself.

"Yes! People sell so many different types of food, and there's this man who sells octopus that always tries to climb out of the jars."

"That sounds *amazing*," she said, her silk sleeves fluttering as she clapped her hands together. I watched her closely. Her geta clacked lightly on the stone path as she stepped out from behind the gate, a stark contrast to my dust-covered straw shoes. The guards glanced at one another again, but didn't move to stop us. Hanako caught the hesitation in their posture and turned her head slightly.

"Is something wrong?" she asked the guards, her voice lilting but with just enough edge to remind them of who she was.

The older guard cleared his throat. "It's not our place, Lady Hanako. Please be careful."

She nodded, satisfied, and turned to me, eyes sparkling. "Lead the way!"

We started down the path, winding away from the compound and into the streets below. The houses thinned out, and the stone gave way to packed dirt, littered with smoothed pebbles. I could feel the eyes of the town on us—on her. No one ever saw someone like Hanako down here. Her kimono was too bright, too clean, her hair pinned just so with ornaments that caught the morning sun. Next to her, I must have looked like a stray dog, all elbows and dust.

Hanako was too busy to care – she oohed and aahed over stalls of mackerel and flounder, not noticing how sparse and empty the trays were.

"Oh my goodness. What is this?" Hanako stooped down and picked up a carved wooden bird. The figure was rough and rudimentary, but Hanako held it like it was a fragile crystal, not a piece of wood.

"Uh, that's a wooden bird. If you want to buy it, Mr. Yang runs this stall," I explained, gesturing to the wary-looking man. He was an old man, and was known to hate the Japanese, although he didn't show it. Mr. Yang had his crooked back brushing against the back of his stall, still glaring at Hanako through his crow's feet.

"So, what about this one?" I asked, holding up a whittled dog. My heart hammered in my chest, and my thoughts screamed, 'Everyone's watching! This is the end of you! Might as well throw away an already ruined reputation! Oh, the shame!'

"That one is cute too!" Hanako exclaimed.

"How much for this one? Is this enough?" Hanako pulled out a small drawstring purse and then proceeded to pour out a small handful of silver coins.

My head spun, seeing all of those shiny pieces fall out of her bag. Mr Yang seemed equally appalled, because he dropped his walking stick and opened his eyes all the way, which never happened.

"So, mister? Name your price." Hanako said, spreading the coins out like it was no big deal. At Hanako's voice, Mr, Yang hardened again.

"Soojin-a, tell this dictator that I don't want her money," Mr. Yang growled, picking up his walking stick.

"Um. Hanako, Mr. Yang says this is too much," I explained to her, grateful that she didn't understand Korean.

"Oh! Um, then, I don't have any other currency…" She said, sadly placing the whittled dog back on the table.

"You know what? I'll buy it. It can be a friendship gift!" I said quickly, pulling out a handful of my father's tobacco from my skirt pocket. Favors, items, and food were most traded for at the market, and Mr. Yang, an avid smoker, was sure to accept this.

"Mr. Yang, please, I just need this one thing," I pleaded, feeling bad. Hanako still looked surprised and partially hurt from Mr. Yang's previous reaction.

Roughly grabbing the tobacco from my outstretched hand, he motioned for Hanako to take the dog.

"Do you like it?" I asked Hanako, who was clutching the piece of wood fondly.

"I love it! Thank you. What else is there to do?" She asked, looking around eagerly.

"We could go see the squids. I used to watch them every day," I said, leading her down the path. My anxiety still raged inside of me, and my thoughts bounced around everywhere. I could feel heated glares radiating from every side.

"Oh, my heavens! How outrageous!" Mrs. Lee hissed.

"My thoughts exactly! Does Mr. Sun know? Oh, he must," Mrs. Kim exclaimed, then was shushed by Mrs. Jang. "Quiet! They're nearing us. But my, my, the Sun daughter, out in public with that glorified moneybag."

"Goodness. I must tell my sister!" Mrs. Cho said, waving her daughter over.

"Saeun-a, go tell your aunt about *that* girl. But, make sure Sun Jun or their father doesn't find out. God knows what might happen to that poor girl if her family finds out." Mrs. Cho shooed her daughter away, and the group of women started chattering again.

As Cho Saeun walked along the path, she stole a glance at Sato Hanako. '*She certainly dresses fancy. But why Soojin?*' Saeun glared at the two of them. '*I thought Soojin was smarter than that. How does someone do that to their rep-*'

"Ouch!" Saeun exclaimed, rubbing her shoulder.

"Move, peasant." A cold voice said in Japanese. Looking up, Saeun was face-to-face with a handsome young Japanese man in a fancy-looking suit.

"O-oh, I'm very sorry," Saeun stuttered in her broken Japanese.

"A slave like you should know better. At least know the language of your masters," The young man frowned and glared as though he had a bad taste in his mouth.

Saeun bowed her head and hurried along, her face on fire. Nearing her aunt's cottage, she walked faster. In front of the old wooden door, Saeun burst into tears.

Hearing her niece's sobbing, Saeun's aunt opened the door.

"Goodness! Saeun-a, what's wrong? Come inside!" Saeun's aunt guided the crying girl to the one chair in the house. As Saeun glanced back, she caught a glimpse of a black suit rounding the corner.

"These squid are so interesting!" Hanako squealed as she jabbed at one of the pink squid's tentacles with a stick. Mr. Woo, the seller, flinched. Everyone in town knew that strange Mr. Woo preferred being with his beloved squids more than interacting with other people, and seeing Hanako jab at them was surely torture.

"Haha... um, do you want to go look at Mrs. Ahn's flowers?" I asked, giggling at Hanako's childish behavior.

"Sure! One second," Hanako was trying to untangle the twig now wrapped in the squid's tentacles.

Suddenly, a shadow fell on us, and when I looked up, I took a startled step back. In a crisp black suit, there stood a tall young man with fair skin and piercing black eyes. I blushed slightly, surprised by his handsome features. He wrinkled his nose at the squids, then glared at me. Shocked, I took another step back, bumping into Hanako.

"Haha, Soojin look…" Hanako paused and turned beet red at the sight of the young man. She shot up and straightened her hair.

"Um hi! I mean, hello, Atsuo." Hanako stammered as she tucked an invisible strand of hair behind her ear. Atsuo, the young man, looked at Hanako coolly, and without even acknowledging her presence, said, "What are you doing?" saying it more like a statement than a question. With one look, he sent trembling Mr. Woo scampering away.

"Well, I was just checking out this–"

"What's this?" Atsuo cut her off and jerked his head towards me. My jaw dropped as I realized I was the "this." Angered, I decided to say something.

"Excuse me," I started, only to earn a look of disgust and belittlement from him.

"Make sure it knows who it's speaking to," Atsuo said to Hanako, not even acknowledging me. I was speechless, looking at this man who seemed to suck the life out of everything around him. Much to my shock, Hanako looked as if she had just met the love of her life.

"Oh, of course," she said, seeming to be in a trance.

"How is your father, Hanako-chan?" Atsuo asked, looking at her indifferently. Hanako stared at his face and quickly looked away.

"He's doing fine, thank you for asking," Hanako fidgeted with her hands and took a deep breath.

"Atsuo! I-I was wondering if you and your father would like to visit for dinner," Hanako said, unexpectedly loudly. Atsuo's eyes widened, then he seemed to contemplate for a while. Then, with a smirk, he said,

"I would love to, Friday at seven, okay Hanako-chan?" Atsuo touched her hand, then turned and walked away. The crowd of villagers instantly parted to make way for him.

I turned to face Hanako and found her staring into the distance.

"Hanako? Hanako!" I said, shaking her.

"What? Oh! Oh, Soojin, did you *see* that?"

"What, him totally disrespecting both of us? Who even was that?" I said, indignant.

"He's Atsuo Gin. One of the imperial advisor's sons."

"What's an imperial advisor's son doing here?" I asked, still mad that he had dehumanized me.

"He's—actually, I don't know why he's here," Hanako said, looking temporarily confused.

"But anyways, that's beside the point. He's coming over for dinner on Friday! You *have* to help me get ready before he comes over," Hanako squealed, grabbing my shoulders.

Suddenly, I realized something.

"Hanako, you don't like him… do you?" I asked, scared of what her answer could be.

"Um, Soojin, I'm only telling you because you're my friend, but… I think he's *the one!*" She exclaimed, smiling, then turning red. My brain momentarily stalled.

"What?!" I exclaimed, shocked.

33

"What do you mean, *the one*? He's horr- I mean, why do you like him?" I caught myself before I offended her. I couldn't understand how Hanako was head over heels for this man.

"Well, our families have known each other for a while, and me and Gin basically grew up together," Hanako said with a boasting air.

"I know he seems a little bit cold now and then, but sometimes you get to see his smile," Hanako sighed dreamily. I was beginning to become increasingly worried.

"Also, did you not see his handsome face? All the girls back home would just *die* to catch a glimpse of him walking through the courtyards!" Hanako exclaimed.

"Oh," I simply said. I knew it wasn't worth trying to reason with her, and I was pretty sure Hanako was just going through a phase.

"Didn't you think he was handsome?" Hanako asked, staring at my face.

"Um, I guess he was pretty decent looking," I said, not wanting to feed the flame. I desperately wanted a change of topic, mostly because I was still mad about his rudeness towards me.

"Well, anyway, I really wanted to go check out the radish stall. You know, the old lady who runs it sometimes carves her extra radishes into really interesting sculptures." I pulled Hanako along, ignoring the glares of my neighbors.

Hanako let herself be tugged forward, the sleeves of her crimson robe billowing in the wind like the banners strung between rooftops. She was still talking about Atsuo—something about the way his hair caught the sunlight—but I was only half-listening. My focus was on the crooked wooden sign that marked the old radish stall near the corner of the village square.

The old woman who ran the stall, Granny Baek, sat hunched on her stool, carefully shaving a plump white radish into the shape of a peacock. Her gnarled fingers moved with surprising grace, each flick of her knife revealing soft feathered lines and arching details that made the vegetable look almost alive.

"Wow," Hanako whispered, eyes wide. "That's amazing."

Granny Baek looked up, the corner of her lip twitching. But when her eyes landed on Hanako's clothes—and then on me, standing beside her—her expression hardened.

"You've got nerve, bringing her here," she muttered in a gravelly voice, returning to her carving.

"Granny Baek, we just came to look," I said, trying to smile.

"I didn't ask for explanations," she snapped. "But you might think twice before parading around with—"

"Please," I said, more firmly than I meant to. I could feel Hanako freeze beside me.

We didn't stay long after that. Hanako bought one of the radishes anyway, placing her coins gently on the table, and whispered a small apology in broken Korean. I could see Granny Baek's hands pause for just a second, as if startled by the gesture. I glanced at Hanako, surprised. I didn't think she would understand phrases in Korean.

We walked in silence for a while after that. Hanako clutched the carved peacock to her chest like a porcelain treasure.

"I... didn't mean to offend her," she finally said.

"You didn't," I said quickly. "She's just—old. And bitter. And scared."

Hanako nodded, but I could tell she didn't believe me.

When we reached the fork in the path that led to the governor's hill, she turned to me with a soft smile. "I'm glad you came today," she said. "I... I don't really have friends here."

"I'm glad too," I replied, even though my heart felt heavy. "I'll see you soon?"

She nodded. Her maids stepped in behind her like shadows, and together they walked away, her crimson sleeves disappearing behind the slope.

I turned to head home, but almost immediately I heard whispers and the sound of familiar sandals slapping against stone.

Hayun and Nari stood near the well, buckets in their hands. They had clearly seen everything.

"Soojin," Nari said first. Her voice was small.

"Wait—can I just explain?" I stepped forward, lifting my hands in desperation.

"You don't have to," Hayun cut in. "We saw you. Laughing, smiling. With her. *Again.*"

"I told you, she's not what you think. She's kind—she helped my father, she—"

"She's Japanese." Hayun's voice was sharp and final. "They burned my uncle's shop, Soojin. He still can't use his arms. How can you just forget?"

"I haven't forgotten anything," I whispered. "But she's not like them—she's—she's different."

Hayun gave a dry, humorless laugh. "They're all the same. You'll see."

Nari looked at me with wide, uncertain eyes. "Maybe you're just confused," she said softly. "Maybe you'll come back to your senses soon."

I gaped at Hayun, whose back was now turned to me. Never in my entire life had I heard her speak and act in such a manner.

They turned and walked away, leaving me standing in the dust.

By the time I got home, the sun had dipped low, casting amber light through the trees. The smell of smoke and broken wood from the ransacked house still hung in the air. My feet ached, and my head throbbed from the weight of the day.

But when I approached the porch, I stopped in my tracks. My father and Jun stood blocking the door. Neither of them moved. Their expressions were stone.

"What's going on?" I asked, wary.

Jun stepped forward. His eyes blazed. "Where have you been?"

"I—I was out. Just walking," I replied, swallowing hard.

"With her?" he spat.

My heart dropped. "You... know?"

"You think we wouldn't find out? People talk, Soojin. You think your little secret friendship wouldn't reach us?" He was yelling now, his voice echoing off the surrounding hills.

"I didn't mean to—she's not like the others, she helped—"

"She's the enemy," Jun roared, fists clenched. "You brought shame to this family. Do you think Mother would have wanted this? You dishonor her memory!"

"Jun," I pleaded, "please..."

But he turned away, shoulders shaking. My father still hadn't said a word. He just stared past me, jaw tight, hands trembling on his cane.

He didn't speak. He didn't have to. The silence said everything.

Jun stepped aside just long enough to reach inside the door and toss out my sleeping mat. It landed at my feet with a dull thud.

"You can sleep outside tonight," he growled. "You want to leave this family? Fine. Start now."

He shut the door with a bang.

In the morning, the light broke slowly across the sky in pale streaks of gold and blue. My bones ached from the cold, but the silence felt louder than anything else. I stood and stretched my sore limbs, hoping to sneak inside before Jun woke up. But as I opened the screen door, I found the main room empty.

No blankets. No bowls. No crutches.

A folded scrap of paper lay on the hearth.

I ran to it and unfolded the message with trembling hands.

Gone to the coast. Don't follow.

Jun

I sat on the cold floor, clutching the note. Now I really was alone. My father was probably with his friends, Jun obviously didn't want to see me, and Hayun and Nari were out of the question.

As I sat on the floor, I realized that I really didn't have anyone to blame but myself. I knew my father detested the Japanese, yet I had unknowingly brought him to his enemy's home. Even after Jun's harsh reprimand, I had spent time with Hanako, and even let myself be seen in the town square. My own foolish desires had gotten me into this place.

I sat in silence for a while, feeling sorry for myself.

That night, after the note and the silence, I curled up by the hearth. The warmth of the fire did little against the cold that had settled inside my chest. I didn't sleep much—just closed my eyes and waited for morning.

When the sun finally crept into the room, my father was already awake. He sat on the wooden bench near the window, staring out at the trees. His hands rested on his cane, and for a long time, he said nothing.

I sat up slowly, unsure if I should speak.

"Come here," he said at last. I obeyed.

He didn't look at me when he spoke. "You think this is about a friend. About a girl with kind eyes and soft words. But you don't know what they've done. What they're still doing." I stayed quiet. I had no defense.

"They burned the rice fields last spring because someone carved the Korean flag into a fencepost. That same week, a boy just a few years older than you was found floating in the stream. Jun knew him." I looked down at my hands. I had heard whispers, but never the full truth. Not like this.

"Your brother..." His voice caught. "Your brother helps us. Quietly. Carefully. So, others don't have to die like that boy did. And you—you walk through the square with the governor's ward like you've forgotten everything." I opened my mouth, but nothing came out.

"I don't say this to punish you," he said, finally looking at me. "I say it because you are my daughter. And I would rather lose your trust than bury you." He stood and left the room, his cane thudding softly against the floorboards.

Later that day, I found a scrap of paper under my pillow. Jun's handwriting.

I'm sorry for yelling. I was scared. Not just for you. For all of us. Meet me at the bridge, after dusk. –Jun

That night, the sky was a deep navy, stars flickering like old lanterns. The bridge by the creek was quiet, save for the rustling leaves. Jun stood there, arms crossed.

"I didn't know," I said, barely above a whisper.

"I know you didn't," he replied. "But that doesn't change what's coming."

He told me everything—about the resistance, about their efforts to protect what little we still had. How he'd lost friends. How he couldn't bear to lose me too.

"I thought after what happened to Mother, you'd understand why we can't just forget."

"I haven't forgotten," I said. "I just—Hanako was the only one who didn't look at me like I was made of glass."

Jun's expression softened. Just a little. Before either of us could say more, a boy from the village came sprinting down the path.

"They're coming," he gasped. "Soldiers. They say someone gave them names."

Jun's face darkened. He turned to me. "Did you ever tell Hanako where we live?"

I froze. I remembered her tracing the town map with one pale finger. Asking which houses were closest to the market.

Laughing when I warned her about the steep steps behind our home.

"Just curious," she'd said.

I didn't answer.

I ran. Back through the woods, past the fields, up the hill to the governor's mansion. The guards at the gate barely glanced at me. One of the maids met me at the door.

"Miss Hanako is ill," she said with a practiced smile. "She won't be seeing guests for some time."

"But I—please, I need to speak with her. It's urgent."

The maid's smile never faded. "Good day, miss."

As she turned to leave, I spotted something on the veranda. The carved peacock Hanako had clutched like a treasure—it lay cracked in two, its beak chipped, tail feathers splintered. At that same moment, I knew, Atsuo was likely being greeted inside. The dinner I'd promised to attend was still underway. Hanako would be in silk and grace, offering him tea with a smile.

And when I didn't come, she'd shrug and say I must've forgotten. She'd act surprised, but only just enough.

By the time I returned home, dusk had turned to full dark. The road was quiet—too quiet.

Then I saw the soldiers. Lanterns in hand, rifles slung across their backs.

I ducked behind the garden wall just as they began pounding on our door. My breath came in shallow bursts. I couldn't move. Couldn't speak.

The door opened. I heard Jun's voice, firm but calm. Then my father's, hoarse and low. I peeked through the leaves. They were dragged out—Jun fighting, my father stumbling behind.

"Where is she?" one soldier barked.

"She's gone," Jun growled. "She left."

"Oh, well. Then I guess we shouldn't leave empty handed…" A slithery voice taunted. My blood turned to ice. I would recognize that voice anywhere. It was the Japanese captain that arrested my father.

From my hiding place, I could see my father, gripping his weathered cane in his trembling, white-knuckled hands. My heart ached, knowing that my father's fragile body probably wouldn't be able to take any more abuse.

"Tie them up," The captain smirked, signaling to a couple of guards near him. Immediately, the guards started to restrain my father and brother's arms.

Jun tried to wrestle them off and got a kick to the stomach in return. I bit back a scream as I witnessed my brother doubled over in pain, and my father, who had been knocked out as well.

As I was about to step out to intervene, Jun, struggling against the guard that held him, looked in my direction and discreetly shook his head. Tears rolled down my face, and I had to bite down on my fist to keep from sobbing out loud. I collapsed to the dusty ground, racked with silent cries.

This was the consequence.

After all those days of telling me, and me never listening, this was everything Father and Jun had warned me about.

I stayed hidden until the last lantern had disappeared down the road, until the sounds of boots and barked orders faded into the trees. My legs were numb. My throat burned from holding back sobs. The garden wall was damp beneath my fingers.

Only once the silence returned did I run.

The governor's mansion was alight with soft gold lamps and murmured conversation. I snuck through the orchard, up the stone steps Hanako had once laughed about, and slipped through the side veranda.

Her door wasn't locked. She was sitting on the floor, still in her night robe. Her eyes were red, her cheeks streaked with tears. She looked up when I came in, startled, then ashamed.

"How could you do this? You told me I was safe with you," I said, my voice raw. Extra tears painfully sprang from my eyes.

I stopped speaking when I saw the dead look in her eyes. She looked up at me with no emotion, tears making rivers down her face. She didn't even blink.

"I'm alone now," she said, the flat look never leaving her eyes.

"Atsuo wants to marry my cousin back in Japan," Hanako's voice cracked on the last word, and then she finally started to sob.

She really was just a privileged Japanese brat. Hayun was right, they *were* all the same. How could she think about her own unrequited love even as she got my family arrested?

"How can you say that? It was you, wasn't it?" I said, fighting the urge to slap her. There was no one else who could have made Japanese guards come and take my family away.

"He looked at me and laughed. He *knew* I loved him!" Hanako wailed, choosing not to hear me. I couldn't take it anymore.

43

"You got my family arrested! I might never see them again! My mom is already dead, so who will be with me? My father is already so old and weak, and they could have already killed my brother because of you!" I finally yelled, tears flowing freely again.

I could sense multiple maids peeking in from the doorway, not knowing if it was ok to come in.

Hanako froze, and slowly looked up at me. Her tears had stopped, but her eyes were wide.

"You know, no one has ever spoken to me that way. Not even my father speaks to me that way," Hanako said, face crumpling again.

"Get out." She said her voice cracking. I felt a little bit bad, seeing that she genuinely looked hurt. As the maids guided me out, Hanako sobbed,

"You never showed up, you know. I waited hours for you, waiting to get your opinion on everything. Because that's what friends do."

"Friends don't get each other's families killed." I glared, the ice in my voice surprising me.

"I didn't mean for it to go this far," Hanako whispered, her voice trembling. "It's my fault Atsuo doesn't want me. He said I was too soft. That I didn't know loyalty. That I was just a spoiled girl playing dress-up in a war."

She looked up at me, her face blotchy and swollen. "So I told him. About your father. About Jun. I thought—if I proved something, maybe he'd stay."

I could hardly breathe.

"You handed over my family so a boy might like you?" I said, each word sharp as shattered glass. Hanako winced, but didn't deny it.

"I didn't think they'd—" she started, but I cut her off.

"Do you even hear yourself? People are suffering, and you're crying over a boy!"

She opened her mouth again, but her voice cracked as she spoke. "I'm sorry."

The words were too small. Too late. The maids finally stepped in, hands light but firm as they guided me back toward the hall. Hanako didn't stop them.

"Get out," she whispered. "Just go."

I let them pull me away, but I didn't stop glaring at her until the door shut behind me.

The night air hit me like a slap. I didn't realize how much I was shaking until I reached the gates. My body moved without thought, feet pounding the familiar dirt roads, past the ghost-silent market and shuttered homes. Against the outer wall of my home, I sat and sobbed until the sun peaked out from behind the ocean waves.

There was only one place left to go.

Hayun's family lived above their noodle shop, tucked behind rows of drying radish. I climbed the back stairs and knocked once—then again, harder.

Nari opened the door, eyes widening when she saw me. "Soojin? What—"

I threw my arms around her and let myself cry.

It was Hayun who made the tea. Nari who found the extra blanket. Neither of them asked questions right away.

Only after I told them everything—my hands trembling as I recounted the soldiers, the arrest, Hanako's betrayal—did Hayun speak.

"Soojin, I'm sorry I said the things I said, but right now, we really need to get your family out of jail before anything happens." Hayun walked over, placing a tray of salted fish on a cupboard to dry.

"My mother says that the Japanese have been executing resistance members in horrible ways."

"What?" I said, my head spinning.

"Soojin, your father and Jun are part of the resistance,"

"Wait, that doesn't make any sense! Jun is a net maker's apprentice, and my father is too crippled to do anything like that!" That couldn't be right. My family would never be part of anything like that. Ever since my mother's death, my father had done everything he could to lead a low-profile life. Jun on the other hand, seemed angered by any sense of rebellion that I had.

Hayun spoke again, "You know how Jun is missing the tip of his ring finger?"

"He lost it in a fishing accident, he told me himself," I said, not understanding her point.

"No, he didn't. He cut it off with eleven other people to show his devotion to our independence." Hayun said matter-of-factly. "I know because the members come to plan at my home."

I took a seat on a nearby chair. My head was starting to pound, thinking about all the things that Jun and my father could have possibly hidden from me.

"Wait a second," I paused, "Nari, did you know about this too?"

"Well, not at first, and then once you started hanging out with that girl, Hayun told me. I'm sorry we didn't tell you sooner..." Nari said apologetically.

"No, don't apologize. Jun asked me not to tell you because he wanted to keep you safe. He thought if you knew you would be in danger," Hayun interjected, coming to face me.

I couldn't get over the way Hayun spoke and acted. Before, she had been the shy one, the one who hesitated to speak. Now, it was as if the roles had changed, and it seemed like Nari was slightly scared of her.

"First of all, we need to get your family out before anything happens," Hayun went on, grabbing various items from her kitchen shelves.

"What? How are we going to do that? The Japanese have guards everywhere!"

"I have a friend who works with some of the guards. He'll let us into the prison."

"We might be able to get that far if we're lucky, but there's no way they won't spot us while we're actually inside."

"Well, it obviously won't be easy, but there still is a way. Every day, women from the village bring food to feed the prisoners. The five women who arrive there first are let inside to distribute the food. We just have to get there first, hand out meals for a little bit, and then you and I or Nari will sneak your father and brother out."

"Can't we just all go at the same time? I would feel better if we all went together…" I said, my hands turning clammy.

"No. It would be too suspicious. We have to take one of us and both your father and brother at the same time to avoid getting separated." Hayun tightened a knot, securing a yellow silk cloth around a bundle of lunch boxes filled with barley and boiled soybean sprouts. She hefted the bundle onto her back, not even flinching at the weight.

"What if they catch us?" I asked, feeling slightly faint. My body felt sweaty, but I had chills at the same time. My sleeves stuck to my arms with sweat, and my head felt like it was a block of lead.

"They won't. Here, wrap this around your head. No one will approach us." Nari handed me a piece of cloth. It was what sick people wore when they went out. I obeyed, securing the strip of cloth around my head.

"Okay, are we ready?" Hayun asked, one foot out the door.

"Yes," I answered, gathering courage.

As we neared the prison, Hayun whispered, "Cover your face with your hair. You won't be easily recognized this way."

I slouched down into my jacket and gave a few unconvincing coughs. Even so, the crowd parted for the three of us as it had when Hanako and I had walked through the town square.

As we came to the prison gates, I noticed that most women weren't stepping forward, pushing to be in the back. I realized that no one wanted to be the one to go inside.

Hayun tugged the two of us along, and the women in line made way for us.

48

As soon as we crossed the gateway, the stench surrounded us.

The rotting odor made me instinctively pull back and gag. Hayun grabbed my arm and pulled me through. I kept my eyes downcast and coughed every few seconds to ensure that we would be left alone by the guards. Nari undid the knot on the sack, and Hayun and I handed the containers of food to the hands that poked through the bars of the cells. Many of the weak hands that grabbed at the food were scarred and dirty, and the faces that belonged to them were gaunt.

The men in the cells greedily shoved the barley into their months, not even pausing to chew.

"Little girls like you shouldn't be in here," said a raspy voice. I turned and saw a scarred hand grab Hayun's wrist.

"Sir, let go of my arm please," Hayun struggled to pull her arm away, and she was starting to look scared.

"How insolent..." the man cackled, "Don't you know that respecting your elders is the right thing to do?"

"Ouch! Let go!" Hayun struggled as the prisoners yanked her towards the bars again.

Nari looked up and tried to help, but the hungry hands kept pulling at the sack.

I shoved my armful of lunch boxes into a full cell and ran to Hayun.

"Let go of her!" I said, picking up a stray piece of wood.

"What is a little girl like you going to do about it?" The man laughed, digging his filthy nails into Hayun's wrist.

"I said... let... go!" I yelled, stabbing the piece of wood into the man's hand. He howled in pain and released her. The wood

49

wasn't very sharp, but there was sure to be a bruise that would last him a while. My head cloth fluttered to the ground, and my hair parted to reveal my face.

"Soojin?"

I turned to the voice.

"Soojin, what are you doing here?" I stared at the owner of the voice. Jun. His eyes were black, and there was a long gash running from his temple to chin. He shoved multiple grumbling inmates out of the way and grabbed the cold iron bars.

"You can't be here, Soojin. Get out before they take you away, too," He whispered, hands gripping the peeling bars tighter.

"Where's father?" I asked, ignoring him.

"There, resting. He's been so weak since…" Jun trailed, looking towards the back of the cell. I froze, hands clutching my white skirt.

"Father?" I whispered, standing on the tips of my feet to find him in the mass of people. Finally, I spotted him leaning against the wall. When he saw me, he gave a small wave and struggled to smile. My heart ached. Jun motioned, and father crawled to meet us at the bars.

"Soojin, it's dangerous." He coughed quietly. I crouched so that I was at eye-level with him.

"We're going to get you out. Just trust me," I pleaded, holding both my father and Jun's hand. They were both so cold.

"Soojin, that's a horrible id–" Jun started, but Nari cut him off.

"We're all in this together. Hayun included," Nari said, glancing at Hayun, who appeared next to me.

"You have a plan?" Father asked, making it sound more like a statement.

"Of course," Hayun said, "Hanjun's on standby."

"Good. It's time," Father said, standing up.

Hanjun? My mind flashed to the dimple-cheeked gardener at Hanako's mansion.

Hayun ignited a match with the nail of her thumb, the bright flame contrasting against the dark dawn sky. Just as quickly as she ignited the match, she dropped it on the damp stone floor to extinguish it.

A tall shadow approached me and tapped Hayun on the shoulder twice.

"Move," a low voice said in Japanese. I jumped to the side and looked up. A tall Japanese officer with dimpled cheeks and kind eyes looked down at me.

Oh, it's Hanjun, I realized, breathing a sigh of relief. *Wait, what? Hanjun? What is* he *doing here?* I stayed silent as Hanjun opened the door to the cell.

"Prisoners Sun Young-Jo and Sun Jun are to be relocated to a different prison," Hanjun said in flawless Japanese. Without hesitating, Father and Jun stepped out, and Father resumed his illness act. He coughed, and his entire body racked. His acting was so believable that I ran forward to support him, but with a quick glare, Jun told me to step away.

Hanjun's face turned to ice as he led Father and Jun towards the gates, and Hayun, Nari, and I followed a close distance behind.

As we neared the center of the prison, a middle-aged officer stopped Hanjun.

"Why are these prisoners out of the cells?" The officer asked, glancing at them.

"Higher-ups have ordered a relocation, sir," Hanjun lied without a beat.

"No. Rookies aren't supposed to be moving prisoners. Hmm. Wait, I've never seen you here before. What is your name?"

"Uh, Kenzo, Sir. I transferred here from another division yesterday," Hanjun's voice faltered the slightest, and my breath caught. My eyes widened and my hands began to shake as the officer slowly pulled out his handgun.

"No, you aren't. There was a division transfer a week ago, so there is no reason for you to say that." The officer slowly cocked his gun and pointed it to Hanjun's head.

"Sir… This must be a misunderstanding…" Hanjun put his hands up, and slowly walked toward the officer.

Suddenly, Hanjun dropped low and kicked the guard's legs out from under him.

"Go! Now!" He yelled, and Father and Jun broke off into a sprint. Hayun pushed me, and mouthed, *run!* I sprinted to catch up with my father and brother, but I was lagging.

"Ha! You're one of those Korean vermin, aren't you? You're not going to get out of this so easily!" The officer roared and was back on his feet in seconds. I glanced back, terrified for Hanjun, but he had seemingly disappeared while the officer was on the ground. I turned back around, and father and Jun had pulled even farther away.

"You! Stop right there!" The officer yelled and pointed the gun towards me. I tried to run faster, but it wasn't good enough. I was going to die.

The officer reloaded the gun, and aimed at me, ready to fire.

BAM!

Suddenly, I was on the ground, and there was a spot of blood growing darker on my jacket. I sat up, dazed.

"What..." My ears rang from the gunshot, and when I looked down, I almost fainted from the sight of the blood.

Did I get shot? No... it doesn't hurt though...

I spotted a figure lying close to me. There was a pool of blood underneath it.

"Jun!" My father's voice cut like a blade across the silent prison.

I turned the figure over, and it was my brother, looking deathly pale and blood flowing in dangerous amounts from his abdomen.

No, no, no no no no.

I froze. My mind went blank as I saw spark fade from Jun's eyes.

This was all my fault. I hadn't run fast enough, and Jun had paid for it with his life.

My father hobbled over and grabbed Jun's shoulders. I realized tears were falling from his eyes, and I sat there, dumbfounded. My father never cried. He hadn't even cried at Mother's funeral.

With a single motion, Father pulled out a gun from his cloak and shot the officer in the head.

"Jun..." he whispered, voice cracking like shattered glass. "No... no, my son..." Jun blinked slowly, as if every movement took the strength of a hundred men. His mouth opened, but no words came at first—only blood, dark and thick, staining his lips. I crawled forward, hands trembling violently, and took his hand in mine. It was cold already.

"Soojin…" Jun finally rasped. I leaned closer, my heart splitting open in my chest.

"I'm here. I'm right here," I choked out, tears falling freely, blurring everything. "Please, Jun. Stay awake. Stay with me." He gave me the smallest, broken smile.

"I'm sorry," he whispered. "I wasn't… always there for you. I should've been. You… you deserved more."

"No. Don't say that. Please—don't say goodbye." My sobs tore through me like a storm, and beside me, Father was shaking, holding Jun as if he could anchor him to this world by sheer will.

"I love you both," Jun said. His voice was thinner now, each syllable a struggle. "You and Father. I always did."

"I love you both," Jun said. His voice was thinner now, each syllable a struggle. "You and Father. I always did." Jun coughed, a harsh, gurgling sound that made my stomach twist.

"Listen… Soojin." His eyes found mine one last time. "Get away from here. This place… it'll kill you too. Go. Live. Don't waste it… like I did."

I shook my head, but his fingers tightened weakly around mine. "Promise me."

"I—" My throat burned. "I promise."

Jun exhaled softly. His grip loosened.

And just like that, he was gone.

"No…" I whispered. "No, no, no—"

I collapsed over him, sobbing until my chest ached. My father pressed his forehead to Jun's, shaking, muttering his name over and over like a prayer.

The morning light broke slowly over the prison walls, casting long shadows across the blood-soaked stone.

Jun would never see the sun again. But I would carry his words with me forever.

And somehow, someday—I would get out of there.

The silence after Jun's final breath felt like it could swallow the world.

There were no more shouts. No gunfire. Just the faint hum of cicadas rising with the dawn and the distant crash of ocean waves on the beach's rocky shore.

Father and I sat there with him for a few more moments— longer than we should have. His blood was still warm, soaking into my skirt, sticky and dark against my hands. I don't remember standing up. I only remember the cold emptiness of my brother's absence as we stumbled away from the prison grounds like ghosts, the sky barely lit with the soft purples and grays of early morning.

We didn't speak.

My legs moved on instinct, the way a wounded animal flees from the scent of smoke. Father limped heavily beside me, his breathing sharp and shallow.

The streets were quiet at this hour—Busan still sleeping under the weight of occupation. We passed narrow alleyways full of hanging laundry, the linens swaying gently in the ocean breeze like pale ghosts. A vendor's stall had been left half-covered, stacks of pickled radish jars glinting faintly under the low light.

55

We moved like phantoms through the village, our clothes soaked in blood—Jun's blood—and dirt, and the remnants of everything we'd been through. People who did spot us from behind paper-covered windows simply turned away. Fear had made everyone silent. Fear of the Japanese, fear of being associated with anyone like us.

By the time we reached Hayun's house my legs felt like they'd been hollowed out. My fists knocked on the wooden gate with barely enough strength.

The small wooden lock slid open, and the glint of coal black eyes peeked out.

"Soojin- oh my God- where's Jun…" Hayun asked, pushing the door open wider. She stared at us and realized.

"Jun is gone, isn't he." Nari choked, appearing beside Hayun. My heart broke again, but no tears formed. My eyes throbbed and I felt lightheaded.

As Hayun and Nari silently cried, Father and I waited.

"I'm sorry, we're wasting time." Hayun handed us a bundle tied with a yellow cloth, much like the pack that she had used for carrying the food to the prison.

"What's this?" I asked, my voice sounding like wooden wheels over gravel. I took the sack from Hayun's hands, and almost toppled over from the surprising weight.

"Food and clothes to last you a week." Hayun explained. It cut into my bones, but I didn't complain. The ache was a comfort now. Proof that I was still alive.

"We can't stay long," Father murmured. His voice had aged ten years overnight. "They'll come looking." Hayun nodded once. "Follow the coast north. Stick to the woods when you can. There's an old train line by the fields near the market. Freight cars sometimes stop there—just climb in and hide. It's not safe, but... it's the fastest way out."

I turned to her. "Thank you." The words barely left my mouth.

The sun was climbing as we left Busan behind. I didn't look back.

The journey north blurred into days of quiet endurance.

Father and I traveled mostly at night, sleeping in the woods or inside crumbling shrines. The road was long and steep, winding through fog-drenched hills and frozen rice paddies shimmering in the moonlight. Rain fell for two days straight, soaking through our stolen coats and into our bones.

Once, we hid beneath the floorboards of an abandoned schoolhouse while soldiers passed by on horseback, their boots hammering against the earth like drums. Another time, a farmer fed us roasted chestnuts and said nothing when he noticed Father's limp and the dried blood on my sleeve. "The land remembers," he said simply, eyes clouded with some old grief of his own.

By the seventh day, we reached Gangwon-do. The mountains here stood like ancient sentinels, draped in mist. It was colder than I remembered, though maybe that was just me. Our destination was a weathered hanok nestled in a wooded valley north of Yanggu. The thatched roof sagged slightly in the middle, and smoke curled from the chimney like a greeting. I recognized the place from stories—this was where my grandmother had lived since before I was born.

She opened the door before we could knock, her back hunched but her gaze sharp as flint.

"Took you long enough," she said. Then, her voice broke. "Come in before you freeze to death."

Inside, the smell of burning pinewood and old barley filled the air. I knelt on the ondol-heated floor, muscles trembling, and let the warmth sink in. Grandmother didn't ask about Jun. She didn't have to. Her worn and veiny hands were gentle as she laid blankets over us, and that night, she sat beside Father while he cried into his sleeves, silently, like a child.

I lay awake staring at the dusty ceiling beams, listening to the wind whisper through the rafters. Jun's voice echoed in my memory.

"Go. Live"

But living wasn't easy. Not yet. Maybe not ever.

Tomorrow, we would wake up again.

Tomorrow, we would plant something in this cold, unfamiliar soil.

And someday, I would return.

Epilogue

I woke to the sound of the chickens.

The orange sun rose in the mountains of Gangwon-do, making the lush green cliffs look like they were on fire.

I rose, slipping my white cotton jacket over my dress. As I stepped outside into the crisp dawn air, the chickens greeted me with hungry clucks.

I made my way over to the sack of corn that hung by the back door and spotted a half-whittled swan on the porch. Father had been carving again.

I picked up the bird, and my thoughts turned to the day in the market with Hanako. It had become a few years since then, and the memory, perhaps because I hadn't thought of anything related to her in so long, was already starting to become fuzzy.

I wonder how she's doing now, I wondered. I surprised myself. The last time I thought about her was full of hate and sadness. I knew I never was going to forgive her for what she did, but now, I could understand her confusion and hurt a bit as well.

The rooster pecked at my uncovered feet, demanding food.

"Oh I'm sorry, mister. You must be hungry." I scooped out a couple handfuls of corn and tossed the kernels around the yard.

The flock of chickens scurried all over the place, chasing after their breakfast.

The sun was fully out now, and I could hear Grandmother steaming peas and barley for the three of us.

Suddenly, a loud crash sounded at the front gate, and the chickens looked up to the disturbance. I walked around to the other side of the house, and there stood a young man in a navy blue uniform.

"Are you Sun Soojin?" The man asked, a strong Japanese accent tainting his Korean. My heart stopped and my hands began to tremble. Why was this person here?

"You have a letter, miss." The man said and held out a neat white envelope. I took it, and carefully slid my nails under the red wax seal. My hands were sweating, and I wiped them on my dress before taking the letter out.

The letter was written in Japanese.

"U-um, I'm afraid I can't read Japanese. Are you sure this letter is addressed to me?" I asked politely.

"Yes. I am sure. I will read this out loud," The man cleared his throat and began.

"Soojin, I know it has been a long time, and I understand if you choose not to respond. I just wanted to tell you that I'm so, so sorry for what I did to you and your family. And you were right. I really was just a foolish brat. This is me apologizing to you for everything that I have done. It's okay if you don't forgive me. I know you will probably think this was stupid of me, but I married Atsuo. It's been three years since our wedding, and I'm regretting it. I can't tell this to anyone, but he's so heartless and doesn't speak to me for days. I checked on your two friends Nari and Hayun, and they and their families are doing well. Once again, I'm wholeheartedly sorry for everything I have done, and it might be one sided, but I still want to

consider you as a friend. Sincerely, Hanako Sato. "The officer finished the translation, and then took out a lighter.

As the letter burned, the man said, "Do not fear, miss Soojin, for I am one of Miss Hanako's trusted servants, and would not tell anyone of the contents of this letter."

I nodded slowly, the letter still trembling slightly in my hands. A swirl of emotions coursed through me—confusion, sorrow, relief—but beneath it all, a quiet sense of peace began to settle. Hanako had finally understood the weight of what she had done. She had faced it. She had written it down, in her own words, and offered an apology I never thought would come.

I looked up at the messenger, whose expression was patient but kind. The weight I had carried for so long seemed to shift, just slightly, enough for me to breathe differently.

"Please wait," I said, a small, steady warmth in my chest. "I have a letter to write to Miss Hanako."

Other Works

An Alien Arrives on (a Still-Good Part of) Earth

I see land

spin, the world a merry-go-round,

shaken senseless.

I look up

and almost fall–

the moon pale and brilliant, and

the stars, blinking bright white:

It's nothing

like home, where hazy orange dust clouds the skies,

nothing to look up to, except rust-

colored gas.

But this–this!

Clean and pure, as though

the sky, once a dirty glass cup, has been washed

so that light gleams off its rim.

I see lush green valley, going down, down, slop-

ing into a snaking stream, flowing

into still, wide waters, a lake so clear

birds soaring overhead cannot tell

Which way is up?

Which way is down?

I, too, cannot tell

Aliens Explain Why They Are Visiting Earth

inspired by Andrea Gibson

Because we wanted to see you for ourselves –

Because we saw that you have invented this thing called time,

and we never understood how you could lack the thing you created. Like,

Why don't you just give yourself more time?

Who owns your time?

Because in New York, Earth's heart of money,

you all take the same train, no matter what you do: Wall Street bankers rapping numbers into phones, clown late to a birthday party, window cleaner hanging by a rope.

Because you chase being rich over happy but envy people

who can be content with less. Because you fall in love, red-cheeked and hazy over two-dollar shots of soju in pop up tents of Seoul, and toss away

a lifetime's love for affairs, confusing love itself to be as cheap as soju.

Because we couldn't understand why you write music for people you'll never meet. Why you look at the stars – our stars! – and wonder if you are alone.

Can't you see us?

Because you create abstract art holding your life's meaning,

And others redesign their reasoning –

enough to call a banana taped to a wall a masterpiece.

We wonder if you will ever find us and explain everything we don't understand.

You Love Me

You love me after school, with fruit cut fresh and laundry folded, unasked.

You love me when you laugh at unfunny things I say, like,

"Today, my teacher really annoyed me." So, then I laugh, and you laugh again, at me, laughing.

You love me when we laugh like a sequence of falling dominos.

You love me when you say it's okay that I'm crying about my brother getting to breakfast before me –

I hate coming second, and even more, I hate my embarrassment about this sensitivity that second-guesses every act.

You say you understand me even when I don't understand myself.

You love me as we sit together on our couch, watching a bad TV show we have already seen.

Words have no need, because you know: I'm dreading the mountain of work I have to do after.

You love me when you reach over the armrest and hold my hand to stop me from picking my cuticles, a nervous tic.

And you love me the next morning, a bleary Monday, when I confess quietly that I didn't finish my work

and you close your computer, take my hands, and say: "We'll do better next time."

Unbroken

When Alice's grandfather saw the glimmer in her eyes, he was transported back to his childhood. He could see a reflection of his younger soul in his granddaughter in every way. The same mischievous spark, the same insatiable curiosity that led him to explore hidden corners of the world, now flickered in her gaze. It was as if time had looped back, the years melting away, and the wonder of youth was once again alive in his heart. The old man could almost hear the echoes of his own laughter, blending with hers, as they shared in the magic of the present moment. Her grandfather could feel the pulse of adventure that once drove him, now fueling her every step. And for a brief moment, he imagined that maybe this was the beginning of a new journey—one where she would find her own way, but never quite lose the thread that tied her to him. The circle, he thought, was unbroken.

Unseen

Clara sat in the living room, clutching her stuffed bear, her gaze fixed on the floor. She had tried to talk to her parents, to make them notice her, but each time they simply brushed her off, as if she were a bother. She could

feel the distance growing between them, a gap so wide it seemed impossible to cross. She didn't know what she had done wrong, but whatever it was, it was clear they no longer saw her as their little girl. She stood up, walking slowly into the kitchen. Her mother was there, standing by the sink, her back turned. Clara opened her mouth to speak, to say anything, but nothing came out. She watched her mother's stiff shoulders, the way her hands gripped the edge of the counter and realized with a sinking feeling that her mother hadn't even noticed her approach.

"Mom?" Clara said softly, her voice barely more than a whisper.

Her mother didn't turn around. "What do you want?" she muttered, her tone cold, distant. Clara felt a lump rise in her throat, but she swallowed it down. She had grown used to it— the coldness, the silence. But it still hurt. It still felt like a sharp sting in her chest every time they ignored her, every time they acted as though she were invisible. She stood there for a moment longer, her hands shaking slightly, before she turned and walked out of the kitchen. There was nothing more to say. Nothing more to ask.

Clara walked back to the living room, her eyes brimming with tears, but she didn't let them fall. She had learned long ago that crying wouldn't make a difference.

About the Author

Emma Hael Kim is a young writer and artist who believes stories can open hearts and connect worlds. Her work has been honored by the Scholastic Art & Writing Awards, the American Library of Poetry, and the ACSI Creative Writing Festival. In her debut historical fiction, Where the Sun Never Sets, she weaves a tale of friendship and betrayal, exploring how light can still be found in even the darkest chapters of history.

When she is not writing, Emma fills her days with painting, music, and community service—sharing art to support children's hospitals, designing educational posters for underserved communities, or playing cello to bring comfort to nursing homes. Whether on the page or in the world around her, she hopes her creativity can plant small seeds of hope and kindness.